NO HOLDS BARRED

SMOLDERING RUINS

NO HOLDS BARRED

SMOLDERING RUINS

Giles Hovseth

Synecdoche Publishing

Smoldering Ruins
Copyright © 2016 by Giles Hovseth.

For information contact:
Synecdoche Publishing
synecdochepublishing.wordpress.com

Edited by Amanda Hovseth
Cover design by Tiffany Schank
Book design and interior artwork by Amanda Hovseth

ISBN: 978-1-945018-05-3
Library of Congress Control Number: 2016915207
First Edition: 2016

≈ *Dedication* ≈

Dedicated to that poor bastard whose laptop I stole, and all my accomplices along the way who helped me monetize my thievery.

You know who you are.

ABOUT "NO HOLDS BARRED"

On August 17th, 2014, I was walking to my General Physics class when I stumbled across a laptop belonging to a man named "Ax Wallace". I've never met the man before, and I don't believe I ever will. The more I have searched for him, the more convinced I have become that he does not even exist. "Ax Wallace" appears to be a pseudonym for some poor stranger who will never find their laptop, but it is also clear that this stranger was quite the prolific writer. His laptop hard drive was absolutely filled with story after story, all supposedly written by this single man.

Now I should specify, "prolific" does not mean "good". Many of these stories made little to no sense. Many were merely outlines or scatter-brained notes describing basic character traits or things of that sort. And many weren't stories at all, but rather meticulous details of the histories of who-knows-what with odd labels like "Cartoon World" or "Zombie Girl". However, among the gibberish and nonsense, I found some of Mr. Wallace's ramblings to have real value.

I have determined to take those worthwhile sections of his writing and compose them into something readable.

My labor has resulted in the series of books I decided to name "No Holds Barred", because nothing of this man's writing is off limits to me and for some unknown reason he liked to pepper that phrase into any sentence he could.

"Oh, what would you like from the store Grandma?"

"Just get me some milk, no holds barred."

You know, that sort of nonsense. Regardless, the title is apt, as many of these stories contain bizarre and unexpected elements, ultimately joyful to read in their own strange way.

As I delve further into his writings, I will find more and more worth passing on to the world, and you can expect these stories to pull no punches. I should also specify that the only connection I have found between these stories (so far), is their shared author. Perhaps that is the only connection they need. Hopefully you will enjoy reading these stories, as much as I enjoyed composing them.

Thank you for reading,

Sincerely,

Giles Hovseth

THE
STEPFATHER
SPARK

Little Darius Snipes had always been an angry child.

The other kids in his class avoided him because of his temper tantrums, but that didn't bother him much. Other kids just frustrated him. They could rarely keep up with his keen, pre-teen intellect, and their smiling faces convinced him they were too stupid to understand the crappy world they lived in. Only an idiot could be happy when life was composed of disappointment after disappointment.

That's not to say there was nothing that Darius enjoyed.

He enjoyed watching the massive metal machines build the structures that stretched above the thick and daunting forest around him. Their power and dependability impressed themselves upon him, while most of the other things in his life were impressively unreliable.

He enjoyed watching the flames that rose from candles, factories, and the occasional campfire. He fondly remembered watching the smoke trail across the sky from the wildfire that once tore through the countryside around him, and he wished he had gotten to see the blaze in person. Even the news footage of cities wrecked by battles between Super criminals and Coalition heroes brightened his day as small fires would sprout up in the debris. The warm lights lifted his heart, and he admired the destructive force of the intense heat that reflected his inner turmoil. The fire in his mind would never settle, and sometimes in the grips of his anger Darius imagined seeing the dark skin on his hands turn a deep red, his clenched fists preparing the blood that pumped inside them to ignite with prepubescent fury.

He also enjoyed spending time with his mother, Kiyana. Or rather, he used to enjoy spending time with his mother. Ever since she married Cassius, she had become a lot less fun to be around. As Darius glowered at the glove box in front of him, his mother lectured him about listening to the school-mandated psychiatrist.

"You can't keep hitting people, honey," she said. "Remember what he taught you. The next time you get angry just breathe in and breathe out."

Darius groaned. She didn't understand. He used that technique at home all the time, but it only worked there because it had to. "Breathing can't solve everything, Mom."

"Well punching doesn't solve anything," she replied.

"It does for Cassius," he jabbed.

Kiyana went silent. Darius could tell through his peripherals that tears were forming in her eyes and falling onto her nurse's scrubs. He felt a sting of guilt. Not even she could control what Cassius did. The man's fists moved faster than either of them could see coming.

"Are you saying you want to be like him?" she asked.

"I'm nothing like him!" Darius snapped.

"Then you need to control yourself."

Darius glared at his backpack on the floor of the car. She just didn't get it. He always had good reason to hit

3

people. Cassius hit because he was a total drunken jerk-wad. It was obvious to anyone with a brain how different they were.

"Well?" Kiyana said.

"Well what?" grouched Darius, turning to his mother with a frown.

"Are you going to control yourself?" she asked.

He grumbled and turned to look at the pavement out the window. The car pulled into a parking spot in front of their apartment complex. It was a nice place, but a recently announced increase in rent prices would soon make their home unaffordable.

"Darius, look at me," she demanded.

He turned back to his mother, the fire in his eyes muted by her stern command.

"Tell me you will try and control yourself," she said.

He broke eye contact and took a deep breath in. "I'll try," he mumbled.

"What was that?"

"I'll try," he said.

"Good," said Kiyana, turning off the engine. "Now let's go inside."

Darius picked up his backpack and stepped out of the car. Closing the car door behind himself, he took his time sliding his arms through the loops of his backpack. He always dreaded the walk to his apartment. Every step he took up those three flights of stairs brought him closer to his step-father.

He heard the trunk shut behind him, and turned to see his mother carrying the usual case of Heineken and a bottle of Hennessy. He remembered a few months back when she asked him to help her carry the booze. It was a costly mistake, and she hadn't asked him again.

He took a deep breath in and forced himself to follow his mother up the stairway to hell. Her breath was ragged when they reached the top, and he ground his teeth as his mother set the case down and pulled the keys from her purse.

Darius watched her switch the lock, and push the door open. The pungent smells of alcohol and body odor rushed into his nostrils. The theme song to *Cops*, a new TV show, rang into his ears. The jerk was home.

Darius took a deep, putrid breath in and let a deep breath out. His mother picked up the Heineken and entered the apartment, and he followed her lead. He was unsurprised to see the back of his step-father's head lounging off the side of the couch, his Jheri curl sagging towards the ground. Cassius Martin laid there every day without fail, and the empty bottles scattered about the ground weren't unusual either.

Kiyana picked up the empty bottles every evening, so Darius knew he could count the new additions and know exactly what kind of night it was going to be. As he untied his shoes and slid them off, he saw ten bottles strewn about the carpet. He glared at the back of Cassius's head. It was going to be a crappier night than usual.

"Is that food ready yet? I've been smelling it all day," slurred Cassius.

I'm not sure how you can smell anything, thought Darius, as he snuck a glance at the TV. It looked like the episode that was playing followed Coalition forces on a routine drug bust. Apparently some people with the power to speed the growth of plants had been farming warehouses full of weed. Officer Slice, a man with the ability to morph his hands into blades, had been sent to make the arrest. Sometimes Darius could understand why *Cops* was

Cassius's favorite show.

"The food's close," said Kiyana from the kitchen.

"Well hurry it the fuck up!" shouted Cassius.

Just like that, Darius could feel his blood boiling. With a final glare at his step-father, he walked to his bedroom and firmly shut the door behind himself. He took several deep breaths before sitting on the floor and pulling his Pre-Algebra textbook from his backpack. He stared at the equations on the paper before him, but he couldn't focus. Instead, his mind wandered down the well-trodden corridors of his pre-teen revenge fantasies.

Darius's pulse quickened as he pictured drawing a knife across Cassius's jugular. His eyes lit up as he imagined plunging an ice pick deep into Cassius's heart. His hands glowed at the thought of lifting up a hammer and smashing out Cassius's teeth, one by one.

Someday, you jerk, thought Darius. *Someday.*

Through the door, Darius heard Cassius yell, "What the fuck is this?"

"It's pot roast," replied Kiyana, her voice muffled.

"Why the fuck is it so dry?" shouted Cassius.

Darius growled. He heard this argument every single day. There was always something "wrong" with the food, and Darius grimaced every time Cassius brought it up.

"Take it back, and make it right this time!" said Cassius.

Darius heard his mother mumble something, but he couldn't make out the words through the door. *She's asking how he likes it again.*

"What the fuck did you just say?" said Cassius.

Darius's ears perked up.

"I said, what's the point?" cried Kiyana.

Darius's eyes shot wide. *She's standing up to him,* thought Darius, a smile spreading across his face.

6

"What's the point?" shouted Cassius. "What is the goddamned point? I'll show you the goddamned point!"

POOM. The door shook and Darius's eardrums ached from the blast of a sonic boom that tore through the apartment. Following just behind the blast, he heard the snap of bone and the crumple of a body hitting the floor.

Darius froze. He listened for his mother's voice, his mother's tears, his mother's anything to show that she was okay. The only sounds were the muffled sirens echoing from the television. He got to his feet. *She's okay. She's okay. She has to be...*

He walked to the door and reached up for the knob. His hand hovered as he took a deep breath in and let a deep breath out. He turned the knob and pulled open the door.

He met his mother's eyes. Her face looked up at him in pain and surprise, tear tracks marking the sides of her cheeks. It took Darius a second to realize her eyes were cold. It took him longer to process the sight of her neck twisted and her chin resting between her shoulder blades.

His breath grew ragged and scattered. He stumbled step by step to his mother and kneeled at her side. Tears formed in his own eyes, and shock began to turn to sorrow.

CLANK. A bottle hit the floor. Darius's gaze shifted from his mother to the bottle. His vision then tracked to the man who dropped it, the man who stood mouth agape, eyes wide with fear staring at the work of his hands.

Darius's fists clenched and his breath drew short. His mother hadn't died, she was murdered. *He* murdered her. A furnace of fury and hatred unlike any Darius had felt before engulfed his body.

He ignited. His pent-up anger erupted from within him;

a shock wave bursting through the room, knocking Cassius to the ground, and causing the entire building to quake in its wake.

Darius looked at his hands. They were ablaze with rage, his body replaced with fire and lava, magma dripping from his fingers onto the floor. He glanced at Cassius, laying against the wall and staring in terror at a child made of flame. He could tell Cassius couldn't believe his eyes, but the child himself wasn't surprised. The power didn't feel alien, it felt *right*.

Darius stepped over his mother's body and moved toward his step-father, molten hand reaching forward. He grasped the bastard's forearm and shouted, "I'm going to kill you, Cassius!"

In less than a millisecond, Cassius tore himself from Darius and sprinted from the building with extraordinary speed, running in much the same way Darius's birth father had years before.

Having missed his chance, Darius's outstretched hand clenched into a fist. He screamed, his rage spreading jets of flame in all directions. The apartment filled with smoke as the room burned down around him.

He turned to look at his mother's corpse. Her hair had been singed away and her flesh crackled in the heat. His breath turned to sobs as he moved to touch her once again.

His molten hands reached under her limp body and lifted her into a cursed embrace. He watched as the arms that had held him in his darkest moments melted at his touch, the flames of his grief causing her skin and muscle to slough into ash. Her caring crow's feet and the kindly curve of her face disintegrated with his gaze. Even her bones dissipated into nothingness as he clung to any part of her that he could.

Racked with sorrow as tears of molten rock fell from his eyes, Darius could only think one thing. *I will find him, Mom. I will hunt him to my last breath, and when I find him… when I finally get my hands on him, he will pay.*

Even the fastest man alive can only run for so long.

Chapter 1

THE CORRODING CALM

"You sure you wouldn't like something to drink?" the bartender asked the young man who had been sitting alone at the bar for the past two hours.

Darius's strength had grown along with his stature, and his musculature showed through the folds of his T-shirt. His physique drew eyes until those eyes would meet the stern and demanding frown that often accompanied Darius's steely gaze. Sipping from his club soda, he replied, "I have a drink."

"Would you like a real drink?" asked the bartender.

"I want a clear mind when she gets here," said Darius.

"Buddy," said the bartender, "I don't think she's coming."

Darius swished his soda around in the glass, then looked throughout the bar. Several old men drank in a corner booth, laughing about a business deal. Two bikers played pool. A young couple fondled each other near the bathroom doors. It seemed like the perfect place, but Darius resigned himself to his growing suspicion that he had struck out once again.

"I think you're right," said Darius. He lifted his glass to his mouth and downed the rest of the soda in one quick gulp. He pulled his wallet out of his pocket. "How much do I owe you?"

"Don't worry about it, man. Soda's cheap," the bartender said, smiling sympathetically. "Save your money for the next date."

Darius grunted and stood up from the bar, "Thanks." He put his wallet back in his pocket and started to move towards the door. At least free soda was always there to dampen his disappointment.

As he reached the exit, the bartender called out to him, "Don't feel too bad about this, you're a good-looking guy. I'm sure you'll meet plenty of women in the future, and if you smiled more, you wouldn't be able to keep them away."

Darius nodded at the bartender and stepped out of the bar, a sly smirk growing on his face. People always wanted to give him advice on things they knew nothing about. This was the fifth bar and the fifth night in a row where he'd gotten unsolicited commentary on how to increase his appeal. He knew they only wanted to see him with a woman, but he also knew the woman would never arrive.

The cool night air filled his nose with the scents of a blue-collar neighborhood. Bars and barbecue restaurants littered the spare edges of an area dominated by defunct factories, construction sites, and rent-controlled apartment complexes. The haze that clung to the air had become a mainstay of "Old Town", the former industrial center of the bustling megalopolis of Carthage. The city limits of Carthage started 30 miles north of Old Town, but anyone born outside of the city could only be bothered to differentiate between the many suburbs if they needed something specific. He was looking for something specific.

One week before, he had found a newspaper article describing the robbery of a liquor store in Old Town. Most Old Town robberies don't make the papers, but this one had been special. An elderly woman buying her weekly stash of Jack Daniel's had fallen to the floor and broken her hip. The lady decided to sue the store, and the store decided to cash in its Super insurance to pay her off. Unfortunately for them, the insurance company refused to pay the store because the store couldn't prove that a Super had committed the crime, or that any crime had taken place at all. The cashier claimed that a gust of wind and a flash of light sped through the store, knocking the lady to the ground and stealing three cases of beer, but the old lady claimed a negligently unmarked wet floor was the cause of her spill. The incident sparked a firestorm debate about government regulation in issues involving Supers, and what constitutes proof of a Super's involvement in a crime, but Darius didn't care about any of that. While most of the country argued about the burden of proof, the article provided more than enough proof for Darius. Cassius had made his way to Old Town, and Darius was going to find him.

Darius approached his hunt strategically and discreetly. Any indication towards his true goal (however slight that indication may be) could send Cassius running to a new town and a new life. This had happened once before. When Darius was only 16, Cassius had robbed a bank in Des Moines, Iowa. The police never solved the case, but he had come close. With bus money stolen from his grandmother, Darius made his way to Des Moines and started intimidating his way through the Des Moines underworld with threats of burnt homes and burnt faces. Consequently, rumors spread of a black kid tearing through town with some serious fire-power, and Cassius took those rumors as his cue to get gone. Darius returned home empty-handed and spent the next seven years waiting for the bastard to slip up again. Cassius had finally revealed himself, so Darius had to keep himself concealed. Every bar saw a man stood-up, and every patron saw a broken-hearted heart-throb. Cassius couldn't know he was here until the bastard was lying limbless in a pool of his own blood, staring up at the fiery face of vengeance unbound.

Musing on his planned revenge, Darius found himself walking down a road darker than most, even in Old Town. Three young men filled with the angst of the underclass leaned against a wall. Darius looked them up and down: baggy pants, tank-tops, and backwards caps; side-eyed glances looking for trouble; most importantly, no guns on their waists. He could take these punks. Hell, he would even enjoy a good fight. His pent up aggression could use an outlet from time to time.

One of the teens with a crooked nose and a black baseball cap detached from the wall and pulled a cigarette from his pocket. "Hey man," he said, "you got a lighter?"

"I don't smoke," Darius replied with gravel in his voice, muscles tensing in anticipation.

"Tch. Alright then," said the teen, leaning back against the wall.

Darius frowned. Were these guys really not looking for a fight? "We got a problem?" asked Darius. Maybe if he pressed them…

"Nah, man," said the teen. "We good."

Well shit, thought Darius as he continued on his way. It had been far too long since he had felt the crunch of bone collapsing beneath his fists. For a long time he could get regular sparring matches at his local MMA gym, but for the past few months nobody had been willing to face him. He wasn't even a particularly skillful fighter, he just hit a little harder than most. He probably went a little further than most too. Now even some punk kids wouldn't pick a fight with him. How else was he supposed to vent his frustrations?

As Darius continued down the street and turned the corner, his wishes were quickly granted. A 9mm handgun was pointed at his face. "Give me your wallet," said the stick-up man.

Darius looked his burglar up and down. Skinny, twitchy, crazy-eyed, and dark-skinned. Nobody would care if he left this man in the gutter.

"I don't have a wallet," said Darius, stalling for time. Which takedown was the most satisfying? Normally, he would unleash a blast of fire, knocking the gun out of his assailant's hands, but fire would give him away.

"Nah, man, I'm not buying it," said the gunman. "You got clothes without holes in them, and you look like you've been eating. You've got a wallet, now give it to me."

"I said, I don't have one," he repeated, pressing his temple against the barrel of the gun. This man wouldn't pull the trigger, Darius could see the fear building in his eyes.

"N-nah man, I don't buy it," said the gunman, turning the gun on its side (and as Darius noticed, taking his finger off the trigger). "I ain't playing with you."

"That's a shame," said Darius, "because I'm playing with you."

Darius's hand flashed upwards, grabbing and twisting the mugger's wrists, causing the gun to fall to the ground. He waited a second to see the gunman's eyes go wide before slamming his fist full-force into the gunman's jaw, then bringing his knee crashing into the gunman's elbow, snapping the arm in half. If the gunman had been conscious as he fell to the ground, he would have been screaming in pain. Darius wished he could hear those screams, but seeing this man's crumpled body lying on the ground would have to be enough satisfaction for now. Screams would have drawn unwanted attention.

With a final glance at the broken gunman, Darius sped his way down the street. Most residents of Old Town would refrain from calling the cops, but he couldn't be too careful. The sooner he returned to his motel the better.

He had managed to find a room at the "luxurious" Starlight Motel, as described by its flashing neon sign. People would come and go at all hours of the night, and the rates were outrageous, but he had been able to charm the desk clerk into giving him a nightly rate instead of an hourly one. Even with a substantial discount, the room cost him more than he would normally be willing to pay, but the location was unparalleled in convenience.

As Darius approached the door to his room on the second floor, he looked across the street at Marty's Discount Liquor Mart. He knew the old "returning to the scene of the crime" trope was largely false when it came to thieves, but he could only hope Cassius would defy the norm, being a drunk, lazy, arrogant piece of shit. If anyone thought he could pull off a second robbery after botching the first, it would be the man who moved faster than he could think. Darius kept waiting for him to return, after all, Marty's Discount Liquor Mart was his only lead. If Cassius didn't return sometime soon, Darius would have to find more permanent lodging to continue his search.

Darius jiggled the room key in the motel lock. He had been staying in this room for close to a week and observed that the only people who couldn't get into these motel rooms were the people renting them. If the door didn't automatically lock, he would have left it unlocked, even in this crime-ridden neighborhood. Nothing he had in the motel was valuable; just a few sets of clothes he got from goodwill, and a couple copies of his welding credentials in the off-chance that he needed to get some odd-jobs to fund his hunt. He had enough money saved up to last a good while, but he didn't expect this shit-hole motel to charge him as much as they were.

This fucking door, thought Darius, the key still loose in the lock. *Why can't these greedy bastards just get keycards? They must be able to afford an upgrade.*

Frustrated, Darius tore the key from the lock and pressed his thumb against the keyhole. His ire concentrated upon the print of his thumb, he poured a pinpoint flame directly into the core of the lock. The melting metal made malleable in his hands, he turned the lock and finally stepped into his room.

The disheveled covers on his bed told him the maid hadn't entered his room. The open suitcase filled with clothes told him nobody else had been in his room either. *Good.*

Darius plopped himself down on the bed and removed his shoes. Despite the musty smell, rough fabrics, and lumpy mattress, he welcomed the rest that came with this shifty bed. Even the bed bugs couldn't disturb him, since they were now dead bugs. It always helped to be your own portable heat treatment. Insects could never hope to withstand the furnace of heat he used to sanitize every new room he stayed in. Even without flames, he could emit intense heat at will. Mostly he used this ability to make fat people sweat when he was stuck with them on elevators, but sometimes he found one or two practical uses for it. The same went for his ability to see infrared radiation.

Mostly Darius used his heat vision to see the fine forms shifting beneath women's clothing, but when it came time to sleep, he found the blurred pulses and fine binary of heat and cold just relaxing enough to lull him off to dreamland.

As he lay back in bed, and his eyes panned across the general infrared uniformity of the room around him, his keenly developed anger retreated to its home deep within his subconscious lying dormant until called to wake again.

In the halfway point between awake and asleep, he noticed the fine pinprick of heat left emanating from the lock on the door. *They're going to make me pay for that... Shit.*

Chapter 2
THE TANTALIZING TRAIL

*B*wampbwampbwamp.

The sound of an alarm stirred Darius from his slumber. His hand instinctively fell on the clock resting on the nightstand beside him.

Bwampbwampbwamp.

Not the clock? thought Darius, his head still groggy with sleep.

Shit, not the clock! thought Darius as he jolted from his bed.

He jumped to his feet and sprinted to the window, pulling back the curtains to see the night sky.

No flashing lights, no sirens. *No cops.*

Whatever happened had only just ended.

No crowd gathering. No one running away. *Business as usual…*

Whatever happened didn't concern the locals.

…Maybe.

Glancing across the street, Darius saw the door to Marty's Discount Liquor Mart hanging off its hinges, angled into the store.

Fucking, maybe.

He rushed to his motel door and yanked it open as fast as he could.

BWAMPBWAMPBWAMP, the store alarm wailed.

The sound was calling him, now was his chance.

Darius sprinted from his door, vaulting over the railing

of the second-floor balcony. He hit the ground with enough force to hurt a normal person, but he was not a normal person.

He rushed through the parking lot and dashed across the street, not bothering to look for cars that weren't coming from either direction.

Come on, come on, let it be him.

Darius stepped around the jagged pieces of the wooden door snapped in half, the alarm bell blaring above his head. As he moved, he noticed the door marked "Pull" had clearly been pushed in. Even a locked door is more easily broken when forced in the right direction. This burglar had either been too stupid to realize this or... *he'd been moving too fast to care.*

The store itself was surprisingly clean and well-stocked. Most of the booze had been left alone, most of the bottles were left unbroken, but only most. Shards of glass lay scattered on the floor in front of two sections of the store; the shelves stacked with Heineken and Hennessy.

Fucking probably.

He bolted back to the door, noticing a jagged section of wood jutting out near the floor. Looking towards the ground, he realized he'd been barefoot the whole time. It was too late to go back for shoes now, but he should be slightly more mindful around dangerous objects like this precarious shard of door. He carefully stepped around it.

Back on the street, Darius needed to be sure. He spotted a high-dollar whore pacing in front of the motel. He shouted at the top of his voice, "Hey Lady!"

"What do you want, honey?" she shouted back.

"Did you see who did this?" inquired Darius.

"Tch. One second it's fine, the next it's not," she said. "I didn't see anything."

Fucking YES! thought Darius.

"So, you want some of this?" said the woman.

"No," he replied. "Thanks though."

"Tch, fuck off with that shit," shouted the woman, but he was too excited to hear.

There has to be a trail. His eyes darted all about the sidewalk looking for some clue as to where Cassius could have gone. Nothing stood out.

There has to be something, thought Darius, frantic for some indication of Cassius's whereabouts. He wouldn't have covered his tracks. He couldn't have covered his tracks. He would have been moving too fast to notice what he'd left behind. *He'd have to be moving too fast to notice…*

Darius rushed to the door and bent down to look more closely at the shard of wood that even he had nearly scraped himself on. Peering at the sharpest point, he noticed an odd discoloration streaked along the side. He pressed his finger against the edge and pulled it back. The liquid was red.

Blood, thought Darius, *still wet and still warm… still warm.*

With fervent inspiration, Darius opened his eyes to the infrared radiation pouring out around him. The shard glowed with the heat of blood that had pumped out at a thousand miles an hour. Fine flecks of effluvia covered a thin streak of the sidewalk and reached into the road. The trail of blood led his eyes to an iridescent footprint that glowed in the center of the road. The hot shine of the footprint could only have been possible through an enormous discharge of energy left through the friction of Cassius's super-speeded feet against the concrete.

Darius ran back to the street and glanced both ways. To the left, nothing stood out, but to the right one heated footprint stretched out beyond another, marks of the man's passing spaced fifteen feet apart from each other. Darius thought about the power that must be present in those legs, but even that power could do nothing to stop him now.

He sprinted down the sidewalk as fast as he could, the sirens of police cars only just then reaching his ears as they echoed in the distance. He imagined that he would soon hear different sirens; sirens sounding the presence of an unearthly inferno that no fire department in the world could have any hope to quell.

After several blocks running barefoot past dilapidated bars and businesses, Darius's breath grew laborious. Staring at the footprints, he noticed that their heat was beginning to fade, his only lead slowly dissipating into the air before his eyes. Running was not going to be fast enough for him.

My car... thought Darius. *Back at the motel. Shit.*

His eyes darted up and down the road. A pair of headlights was speeding towards him.

That works.

Darius stepped into the road putting his hand up to stop the oncoming vehicle. He started to channel heat to his hand, but realized that as close as he was to finding Cassius, any sign of fire could send the bastard running off to God-knows-where. He would have to do this the old-fashioned way.

The tires screeched, grinding the car to a halt in front of him. The car was a beat-up Honda Accord. He was lucky it managed to stop at all.

He walked to the driver's side and yanked open the door. A young woman looked him in the eyes, steel in her gaze and a gun in her hand. She said with a touch of sass, "Are you trying to rob me?"

Darius was surprised by this revelation, but the footprints were fading fast. "I'll pay you $100 to drive me where I need to go."

"A hundred dollars?" asked the girl, eyebrow slightly raised.

"One hundred dollars," replied Darius emphatically.

"A hundred fifty and you drive yourself," she replied.

"Deal," said Darius. This worked better anyways, he wouldn't have to give directions to someone who couldn't see where they were going.

The woman put the car in park and climbed to the passenger seat of the car, keeping the gun on Darius the entire time. He clambered into the driver's seat and slapped the gear into drive. The tires screeched as he slammed his foot down on the gas. The trail was going cold.

"Take it easy, you'll wake my baby girl!" shouted the woman.

Darius looked into the rearview mirror to notice a napping toddler strapped to a carseat.

"Sorry lady, I'm pressed for time," he said gruffly. It was just his luck there would be a kid in the car. Kids always complicated things. He allowed the car to slow down.

"You running from the cops or something?" she asked.

"No," said Darius, "I'm after the person who is."

"Did he steal from you?" she asked.

"Something like that," he said.

The trail turned left, and Darius took the turn a little too sharply. A soft cry emanated from the backseat as a toddler stirred in her slumber.

The woman hushed her child and cooed, "It's okay, Mariah. You're okay."

"Mariah's her name?" asked Darius. He glanced at her in the mirror. *Cute kid.*

"Yeah. Julian and I thought it was a real pretty name," said the woman. "It's a nice white person name. She could get an honest job with a name like that."

"Do you have an honest job?" asked Darius.

"I've got a gun pointed at a stranger who I'm allowing to drive my car for a hundred and fifty dollars," said the woman.

True enough, thought Darius. "What's your name?"

"My name's Tonya," she said.

"I've met a white Tonya before," he said.

"A white Tonya Jackson?" asked Tonya raising an eyebrow.

"No, I guess not," said Darius, taking a right turn. The trail was getting noticeably more difficult to follow. He sped up a little more.

"You got a name?" asked Tonya.

"Dar-" he stammered before realizing he may still need to keep his identity a secret, just in case he couldn't find Cassius tonight. "Do you watch the news?" he asked instead.

"I do, for work," said Tonya.

"Then I'm sure you'll learn my name soon enough," said Darius.

"What kind of answer is that?" asked Tonya.

Darius's eyes shot wide. There were no footprints before him in the road.

He slammed on the brakes, and threw the car in reverse. The tires peeled out as the car sped backwards, and he turned his head to see where he was going. He saw Mariah wailing in his peripheral vision. *Sorry Mariah, I'm too close to take it easy on you.*

25

"What are you doing to my car?" shouted Tonya furious.

He ignored her and kept speeding backwards.

There, thought Darius, as he spotted a footprint barely visible in the road. He slammed on the brakes again, stopping just in front of the footprint. His eyes darted all around his surroundings. On the side of the road stood a collection of run-down condominiums filling up several city blocks. Another footprint softly glowed on the sidewalk leading into the condo complex. Cassius had left the road.

Ecstatic, Darius slapped the car into park and pushed open the car door. As he stuck his foot out of the car, he heard Tonya yell over her crying daughter, "Pay up or I shoot!"

Shit, he thought as he pulled his wallet from his pocket. He ruffled through his cash and brought out the $150. *Two nights motel fare… it'll all be worth it once it's over.*

He threw the money into the car and sprinted towards the condominiums. He heard Tonya yell, "You're welcome!" as the car drove away behind him.

For a moment Darius found himself worrying for the future of that little girl, but all thoughts of other people left his mind when the glowing footprints went from 15 to 10 to 5 to 1 foot apart. The slight increase in heat with these last few footprints indicated a correlative increase in frictional force. Cassius had used this sidewalk as a landing pad.

Darius's pulse quickened. He was close, so very close.

He carefully scanned his surroundings for the heat signatures of people in the area. The infrared uniformity of the block of condominiums gave him nothing good to go on. Cassius must have left some sign of his presence besides a fading heat signature, so Darius allowed his eyes to readjust to the spectrum of light normally visible to humans.

The look of the condos didn't change much. Clearly all built by the same developer decades earlier, each building was two stories tall and had two front doors. In the dark of night, the paint looked black, but it could have been a dark blue. Either way, the paint on each building was chipped and peeling. The buildings had probably never been repainted during all of the years of their sad existence.

Some residents had done their best to liven up their monotonous environment. Lawn decorations cluttered the meager porches the city zoning laws allowed them to have. Wind chimes hung from three or four eaves. Some houses even had children's toys cluttered about the stoop. Darius could safely guess that these condos did not belong to Cassius. The bastard was much more likely to be a part of the majority of condo residents who resigned themselves to the dull and inevitable rot of time. As Darius walked down the street, each condo seemed as likely to house his step-father as the last.

There has to be something, thought Darius, his search extending further and further into the night. That "something" appeared with a sharp and jarring pain as it jammed into Darius's bare foot. Jumping back in shock, he saw a pile of shattered glass strewn about the sidewalk. Lifting up his foot to look at the damage, he spotted a large shard jutting from the arc, blood dripping from the wound. He pulled the shard from his foot, then with firm concentration, he focused his heat on the stabbing pain. A minuscule flame engulfed the cut, and the wounded flesh soon cauterized itself. The gash closed, and the heat healed the harm, restoring his skin to its uninjured form.

Inspecting the ground, Darius noticed the broken glass had once been a bottle of beer. The label, torn in pieces on the ground, still possessed enough integrity to inform him of its manufacturer: Heineken. *This must be it.*

He moved around the glass and up the steps of this condo's porch. A single chair sat upon the porch, along with rows of empty bottles and cans. The evidence grew more damning by the second.

Darius peeked in the window for signs of movement. A television flickered light into a living room housing a ratty old couch with nobody sitting on it. He could see from the light of the TV that the living room was connected to a kitchen, and from that kitchen a backdoor allowed secondary access to the building. Behind the couch, stairs stretched up to the second floor.

Liquid trickled down the stairs. The stream's origin appeared to be a 40 ounce bottle of Hennessy lying on its side halfway up the flight of steps. He remembered finding many bottles arranged similarly during his childhood. Cassius always ended the night with hard liquor, and he would leave the bottles wherever they lay as he would stumble to bed. For the first time in his many years of plotting vengeance, it struck Darius how little the bastard had changed in the past decade. Alcohol was this asshole's only driving force, his only reason for living. Without knowing why, Darius felt a twinge of sadness for the man and his small life. Perhaps his death would come as a relief to the man himself, and not just Darius. Sadness gave way to excitement as he realized just how soon that death would come.

Feeling confident that Cassius would be asleep, Darius reached over to the doorknob and attempted to turn it. The doorknob rotated smoothly in his hand, the door softly squeaking as he pulled it open. Darius didn't remember the bastard being so trusting as to leave his door unlocked, even in his drunken torpor. *Maybe he forgot,* thought Darius.

He stepped into the condominium, taking care to make as little noise as possible. He gently shut the door behind himself, locking it just in case someone tried to enter in behind him or someone tried to get away. His pulse started to race with anticipation. The air was hung with anxiety, and an odd scent entered his nose. Darius couldn't place the exact origin of the smell, but the metallic tinge allowed him to imagine it to be the blood that would soon fill the home, foreshadowed by a simple misstep at the liquor store.

With trepidation, he started to climb the stairs. Step by step, he grew closer to his goal. Tonight could be the night his dreams come true, but one wrong move and he'd have to start the search all over again. Each stair creaked at his ascent. Each breath flowed with quiet precision.

As he reached the second floor, three doorways stood open before him. He peeked into the first, greeted by a modest bathroom that smelled like it hadn't been cleaned in months. The acrid odor hit his nose with a punch, but something about the bathroom smell seemed different from the one that filled the rest of the house. An uneasy feeling started to creep its way into the back of his mind, but he pressed forward, ignoring the possibility of complications.

The next door revealed a room filled with alcohol and odd goods. TVs, t-shirts, posters; the items were haphazardly strewn about the floor with wads of cash periodically appearing between them. A stash of liquor sat by the door, the bottles still full and matching in design with those bottles left on near-empty racks at the liquor store. Darius figured that if Cassius was willing to steal alcohol, it made sense that he would steal other things as well. It was only a shame that these items found themselves among the horde of goods stolen by a man who didn't care to care for them. They may as well have been discarded on the side of the road, but the selfishness of Cassius always came with a possessive neglect. Soon, none of that would matter at all.

Darius moved further down the hallway and turned to see the final door hanging open just a crack. He lifted up his hand, and slowly pushed it open. The strange scent grew even more pungent as the door opened, but it only registered in his subconscious, as the sight froze him in place. There, in the pseudo-twilight of a streetlamp whose light leaked into the window past shutters that hung in disrepair, lay Cassius, sprawled unconscious across his bed, face-down in a pool of drool and alcohol.

Darius couldn't believe his eyes. His fists clenched, and his heart pumped with a force that nearly tore itself from his chest. Over a decade of searching, over a decade of plotting, and he'd found the man in his most vulnerable state. *It's too good to be true*, thought Darius. *Make sure*.

He approached the bed with trepidation. His hand shook as he reached out towards his step-father, gently lifting back the mass of sheets that covered the man's left arm. Beneath the sheets lay the greatest sight he had ever seen: the man's forearm possessed a distinct and awful scar, roughly the shape and size of a pre-teen's hand, if that hand had been engulfed in flame.

Tears of joy filled Darius's eyes. Under his breath, he whispered ecstatic cries of, "Yes, yes, yes, yes, yes," his arms pumping with excitement. A giggling laughter started to creep up his throat. He tried to stifle his laughter, but the elation of the moment was uncontainable. He let out a load guffaw, keeping an eye on Cassius the entire time. Even with all of Darius's excitement, the bastard didn't stir from his slumber, knocked-out cold by the deep sedative power of alcohol.

His joy expressed, Darius allowed himself to catch his breath. Breathing deeply in and out to calm his nerves, the strange smell reentered the fore-front of his consciousness. Now near the source, he could tell that it wasn't blood. Instead, it had the odd tinge of seafood, or something you'd find washed up by the harbor. Unashamed and unafraid, he leaned forward to sniff his step-father. Alcohol and body odor exuded from the man, but the strange scent had to have another source. Satisfied that Cassius's slumber would provide him sufficient time to solve this puzzle, Darius glanced around the room for anything that could be emitting the odor.

He spied a clear path to a floor vent on the other side of the room. Perhaps the smell was being piped in from somewhere else, so Darius began to move towards the vent. Unfortunately, what looked like a clear path was not clear at all.

Halfway to the vent, Darius bumped into a man who could not be seen and had been standing silently watching in the corner of the room. He felt the man's arms quickly wrap around him and a stabbing pain erupt above his collarbone. He tried to throw a punch, but as he fought to free his arm from being pinned to his side, his movement became sluggish and tiresome. His eyelids grew unbearably heavy, and his legs began to collapse beneath him.

As Darius slouched to the floor, his eyes opened to the heat in the room revealing the infrared imprint of a bizarre and blurry sight. In his fading consciousness, he thought he saw a man with a beard that moved like tentacles standing over him, and he thought he heard that man whisper, "Sorry! Sorry, sorry, sorry… so, so sorry."

Chapter 3

THE DIVERTING DIALOGUE

Darius groaned. His head pounded. A spot on his neck burned with an itchy pain. He tried to open his eyes, but the light was too bright for him to handle. In his groggy half-wakefulness, he wondered, *Where am I?*

He knew he was lying down. The ground beneath him felt soft, yet firm. He figured he was on a bed. His hands were stretched over his head. He tried to bring them down, but he soon noticed a constricting pain around his wrists. He was handcuffed.

Handcuffed? What the shit…

Darius forced his eyelids to open slightly. His head still pounding, he realized that his unfocused eyes were allowing too much light to enter his brain. He shut his eyes, thought about the primary visible spectrum, and reopened them. His vision readjusted, allowing him to gaze up at a ceiling marred with water stains, lit by the shaded light of day. He glanced towards his hands. Irregularly large cuffs chained him to the headboard of the bed.

His blurred mind struggled to remember what had happened the night before. He'd been chasing… *Cassius, but then… something. Some… smell?*

He took a deep breath in, a familiar fishy scent greeting his nostrils. *That smell, why that smell?*

He glanced around the room. It was a simple bedroom with shutters on the window and a vent in the floor. The door was shut, but he felt as if he had entered this room before. *Or at least*, he thought, *a similar room.*

He could hear a muffled voice speaking on the other side of the door. He couldn't make out the words, but the sound brought one word to the forefront of his memory, "*sorry*". *Sorry for what?*

Finally, the full memory of the night before pieced itself together in Darius's mind. "Mother fucker!" he shouted, as he slammed his hands forward, the cuffs making a loud clang on the headboard. He banged the cuffs again and again, the headboard refusing to give way. His rage grew with each failed pull. *If it won't break, it will burn.*

As he prepared to ignite, the door creaked open. A timid and nerdy voice spoke over Darius's fury: "Sir? Sir, please calm down."

"Calm down? Calm the fuck down? Do you know what you've done?" Darius shouted, cuffs pulled tight against the bed.

"Sir, I... I know what I've done," stammered the man, "But it's what you've... what you've done that matters."

"What *I've* done?" Indignant, Darius pulled himself up to get a better look at the man who had ruined his hunt. He soon wished he hadn't. "Jesus, fuck! What is wrong with you?"

The man stood awkwardly in the doorway, a flip phone in his hand. He wore only gym shorts, and a pale, rotund belly hung out over his waistband. His most striking feature was a mass of tentacles sprouting beard-like from his face. His eyebrows were cinched together in frustration. "I'm the Cuttlefish."

"The Cuttlefish? What the fuck is that?"

"It's a cephalopod. They're... they're really cool, actually. I'm part cuttlefish," he explained, "I'm the

Cuttlefish."

"Fucking Cuttlefish," said Darius. He pulled at the cuffs again, "Can you explain this to me then, through those dumbass tentacles?"

The Cuttlefish growled, then gruffly said, "You walked into a sting."

"You're police?" asked Darius, surprised.

"Well, no," said the Cuttlefish, "I'm … I'm with the Coalition."

Shiiiit, thought Darius, "The Carthage Coalition?"

"Exactly," said the Cuttlefish, "They… well, *we* believe the man whose house *you* broke into is responsible for a string of unsolved crimes in the area. *I* was running surveillance until *you* walked in and did that goofy dance."

"So you chained me to a bed?" asked Darius, indignant.

"You would have ruined the integrity of the mission," said the Cuttlefish. "Any indication that someone is watching him, and Jamal Murphy takes off, never to be seen again. That's what they told me."

Jamal Murphy, thought Darius. *They don't even know his real name.*

"Wouldn't the smell give you away?" asked Darius.

"Psh," blew the Cuttlefish, his tentacles flapping with his exhalation, "that man's nose smells only alcohol. I've been watching him for days, and he hasn't noticed a thing."

Days, thought Darius. *The first robbery tipped off the Coalition as well.*

"Why the cuffs?" asked Darius, lifting his hands.

"I didn't know what else to do. I'm… I'm kind of new at this," said the Cuttlefish, shaking his head. "I said I was sorry."

"Can you take them off?"

The Cuttlefish looked at Darius, then the cuffs, and looked away. "Sorry, but no."

Darius narrowed his eyes. "Why not?"

"I don't exactly…" stammered the Cuttlefish, "I don't have the keys. I just called my par-… my supervisor. She'll let you out when she gets here."

Darius clenched his fists. He wanted nothing more than to blast his way out of the cuffs, but with Cassius still out there and the Coalition involved, he'd have to keep his powers secret for a little while longer. *Unless they already know.*

Darius stared at the Cuttlefish, searching his face for information. The only thing Darius could tell was that he felt uncomfortable with people looking at him. The heat of Darius's gaze made him sweat.

"These aren't normal handcuffs are they?" Darius glanced up at his restraints again, feigning ignorance. He'd seen this style before. "They're bigger than normal cuffs."

"Yeah," the Cuttlefish chuckled, "They're made for Supers. I would have used regular ones, but those are the only cuffs they gave me."

Darius grunted. *He doesn't know, and Cassius doesn't either. The hunt is still on.* He allowed himself to relax. He needed to strategize. If the Coalition was watching Cassius, he would have to get them off his back just long enough to kill the bastard. He would have to remain vigilant, searching for opportunities.

He looked at the Cuttlefish, still standing in the doorway. *Maybe I've got an opportunity right here.*

"So you turn invisible, then?" asked Darius.

The Cuttlefish perked up. "Oh, yeah. Would you like a demonstration?"

"Sure," said Darius.

The Cuttlefish smiled. His skin started to ripple with colors, and, in a second, he was gone, a pair of shorts floating where he stood.

Darius's eyes opened wide. In curiosity, he switched his eyes to infrared. The Cuttlefish's body heat betrayed him. *Let's see him sneak up on me now*. He smiled.

"Impressive," he said. "You do anything else?"

The Cuttlefish reappeared, "You remember how I knocked you out?"

Darius raised his eyebrows. "I didn't see *how* you did it."

The Cuttlefish chortled, "Cuttlefish venom. Look."

Darius watched as the Cuttlefish opened his mouth beneath his tentacles. A long tube with a sharp and terrifying point slithered out beneath his tongue. Darius's stomach turned as the Cuttlefish wiggled his stinger about, chuckling the whole time.

With a final laugh, the Cuttlefish retracted his stinger and said, "That's my favorite part of the Cuttlefish."

Queasy with the thought of that disgusting stinger having pierced his skin, Darius made another sickening realization: he hadn't seen any floating shorts before the Cuttlefish had grabbed him. Darius frowned.

"You okay?" the Cuttlefish asked.

Before Darius could answer, the sound of a door shutting came from the first floor of the house. A woman shouted, "Harold?"

"Up here!" the Cuttlefish shouted back as he anxiously sidled further into the room.

Feet stomped up the stairs, and Darius watched as a woman turned into the doorway. She was of average height with a wiry frame and long brown hair pulled into a ponytail. Darius thought she looked very similar in age to himself, but she did not look happy as she glanced at him, then looked at Harold with palpable disgust.

"You didn't *do* anything to him, did you?" she asked.

"What?!" said Harold. "No! Lana, I wouldn't... he's... he's a dude!"

Lana growled, clearly holding back some fury of her own. "For the last time, *Harold*, call me Construct." She looked to Darius. "Do you feel okay?"

"I'll feel better once I'm out of these," said Darius, clearing his throat and shaking the cuffs.

"I'll let you out," Lana said, "When I decide to let you out."

Darius's brow furrowed. "He said..."

"I don't care what he said," Lana interrupted. "You walked right into the middle of an official Coalition investigation. As much as I would rather not deal with this, I can't let you walk away."

Shit, thought Darius, as he shot Harold a withering look. Harold shrugged apologetically as one of his tentacles twitched nervously.

"What were you doing in Mr. Murphy's home last night?" Lana asked, moving closer to the bed, staring Darius down.

"That's my business," said Darius returning her gaze.

Lana cleared her throat. "I'm sure it used to be. It's our business now. If you want out of those cuffs, we're going to need some information."

Darius glared at her. *The longer I stall, the more suspicious I look*, he thought. *What can I tell her?*

Lana sighed. "Perhaps I'll start by telling you what we know. That way we can avoid repetition."

Darius didn't appreciate her condescending tone, but he held his tongue.

"We know your name is Darius Snipes. We know you're a welder. We know you aren't from around here," Lana said matter-of-factly. "We know you have a criminal record…"

"No," blurted Darius. "I was a minor. The records have been expunged."

Lana raised an eyebrow. "A bit touchy about that, aren't you Darius?"

"Who wouldn't be?" growled Darius. *I should've kept my mouth shut.*

"We know you have a criminal record," she repeated, somewhat smugly, "and we know that you were trespassing on Jamal Murphy's property. I would also add that you were quite happy to be on Jamal Murphy's property."

Lana moved closer to the bed, leaning down over Darius. Her assertive demeanor annoyed him, but the closer she got, the more he admired the fierceness in her eyes. He had to tell her something.

"So, Darius. Mr. Snipes. Tell us something we don't know," she said. "Tell us why you were so happy to be in that room last night. Why were you there?"

Darius ground his teeth while looking deep into her eyes. He had to think of something she'd believe. *Something "true"…*

He cleared his throat. "Jamal Murphy is my father."

He heard Lana sharply inhale. *She's surprised. Good.*

"He ran when I was born," said Darius, "and he's been running since. Last night was the first time I'd seen him since… well, since he left."

Lana stood up straight and glanced at Harold, who'd been awkwardly standing in the corner. Harold shifted his feet and shrugged.

40

Lana pursed her lips and wiggled her jaw. Her eyes shifted around the room. "His records don't list a son. Are you sure he even knows you exist?"

Darius resisted the urge to grin. "He knows. He just doesn't know that I'm here. If he knew I was coming... I doubt he'd stick around to meet me."

"So you broke into his home, just to say hello?" asked Lana, still slightly skeptical.

Darius shrugged. "I didn't think there'd be a squid crouching in the corner."

"Cuttlefish," said Harold.

Lana shot Harold a withering look, his tentacles twitched in response. She glanced back at Darius. "I'm going to make a quick call. Harold will keep you company for a little while longer."

As she turned to leave the room, Darius said, "You both forgot the keys?"

Lana looked back at him, and curtly said, "I'm going to make a quick call." She walked out the door.

Harold stared at the spot where she'd been, a lurid look in his eye. Darius took note.

"She always bossy like that?" he asked, baiting the fish.

"Huh?" said Harold, pulled out of a daydream.

"Does she usually order you around like that?" asked Darius.

"Always," responded Harold.

"You not man enough to do something about it?" asked Darius.

"I..." said Harold, flustered, "I don't have a choice."

"I thought you said you were partners," said Darius.

"No, I said she was my..." Harold paused. Darius raised an eyebrow.

Harold sighed and lowered his voice before saying,

"She's my parole officer."

He's a felon, thought Darius, a grin forming on his face. *I can work with that.*

"Still," he said. "A man always has a choice. Someone like you could slip away and never be found. What's she going to do about it?"

"It's not that simple," said Harold. He looked towards the door, then moved to the bed next to Darius. He turned his back to Darius and pointed halfway up his own neck. "Do you see this?"

Darius peered at where Harold was pointing. A small rectangular bulge protruded from Harold's skin. Shivers went down Darius's spine. He didn't know the Coalition had the legal authority to install tracker chips into human beings, even if they didn't seem entirely human.

"I don't have a choice," said Harold while turning to face forward.

Darius glanced towards the doorway, still empty. "Might be I can give you a choice."

Harold's eyes widened. Darius continued, "If you can stand a little heat."

"What do you mean?" asked Harold.

Before Darius could reply, Lana's voice came through the doorway. "Okay," she said as she turned the corner into the room. "I'm going to let you out of the cuffs, but you aren't free just yet. Until we capture Jamal Murphy, you are hereby placed into Coalition custody."

Darius tensed up pulling the cuffs tight against the headboard. "You can't do that, I'm not a Super! The Coalition has no jurisdiction over me!"

Lana snorted. "Don't be a baby. Your father's a Super, and you snuck into his home while he was under investigation. We've got all the jurisdiction we need."

Darius took a deep breath in and let a deep breath out. He resisted the urge to burn the house down and instead managed to say, "Will I at least get to speak to him?"

"If we catch him, I'll let you talk as long as you like," said Lana.

Darius breathed in, "What am I supposed to do now?"

Lana smiled. "I'm sure we'll figure something out. Now hold still while I unlock your cuffs."

Darius pulled the cuffs tight and held them still. Lana lifted up her hand and waved it in the air. A key made of ephemeral blue light appeared floating in the air before her. Darius's eyes went wide as he watched the key float towards the cuffs and turn in the locks. The cuffs unlatched and dropped with a heavy clank onto his face.

"Fuck!" he shouted, his nose throbbing with pain.

Lana chuckled, "Hey, at least they're off your wrists."

Darius lay on the bed, groaning and rubbing his face. Lana chuckled for a few more moments before saying, "I'm going to make some coffee. Join me downstairs when you're ready."

As she left the room, Harold watched her go. Darius sat up on the bed, and Harold turned to him, speaking in a low voice, "What did you mean by 'heat'?"

Darius rubbed his nose and responded, "I was being very literal."

Confused, Harold looked out the door and looked back to Darius. "You are talking about escaping, right?"

"I'm talking about freedom," said Darius.

Still confused, Harold reiterated, "The freedom to run?"

"The freedom to choose," said Darius, *to choose who dies.*

Chapter 4
THE
FLAWED
FRAUD

"We need a confession because a confession is what we need," said Lana, turning the steering wheel slightly to the right. The dim streetlights of Old Town periodically shone across the dash. "There's nothing more to it."

"Bullshit," said Darius, scratching at the ankle monitor bracelet that had replaced his handcuffs. The bracelet was high tech and very discreet. If not for the itch, he may not have noticed it at all. "You could get a conviction ten times over with the evidence you've got. This is about sentencing, isn't it?"

"It doesn't matter what it's about, it only matters what we need. We need a confession, so we're going to get one. He needs to tell us about his powers," said Lana emphatically. "If you'd rather not help us, then I can drop you off at the police station, see what they make of breaking and entering."

Darius glanced at Lana as she stared towards the road. He could tell this wasn't her first time blackmailing someone, but she placed too much confidence in her threats. He couldn't care less about picking up a trespassing rap, but he needed to stay close to Cassius, and she had given him the perfect opportunity.

"The Coalition is aiming for a death sentence, aren't they?" said Darius. He already knew the answer, but he liked to see his captor sweat.

"No!" said a startled Lana. "God no! The man's a thief, a death sentence would be horribly inappropriate. We just need a confession to prove it's him, okay? Nobody wants to kill your father."

Darius smirked. "You just need a confession to prove it's him."

"Yes," said Lana, relieved. "That's all we need."

Darius turned his head towards the backseat and raised an eyebrow at Harold. Harold shrugged, then reached up and scratched the back of his neck. *The tracking chip.* Darius grunted in acknowledgement, then turned his gaze back on Lana.

"You really think he'll go for this?" asked Darius.

"Harold's seen him do it before," replied Lana.

"Yeah, he gets competitive over pretty women," said Harold.

Darius noticed Lana shudder at Harold's use of the word "pretty". *I'd be grossed out too if those tentacles found me "pretty",* thought Darius.

Harold continued, "I think Jamal will go full ham when he sees Lana."

Lana gagged, and pulled the car to the side of the road. "Okay Harold," said Lana, "this is close enough. You know how to get there from here."

Harold sighed. "Okay." He waved his hand over his face, and his tentacles faded out of sight, revealing a normal looking, albeit chubby, face. Darius jumped at the sight.

"You can just… look normal?" asked Darius.

"Yeah?" responded Harold, confused.

"Well, why don't you do that all the time?" asked Darius.

"Because my tentacles look awesome," replied Harold.

Darius raised his eyebrow at Harold, who stared awkwardly back. "Look," said Darius, "Brother…"

"Just go Harold," interrupted Lana. "We've got work to do."

"Okay," said Harold, opening the car door. As he stepped out of the car, he murmured, "My tentacles are cool though."

Darius watched as Harold shut the car door and walked into the darkness of a nearby alley. Darius looked back at Lana, whose hands were clenched on the steering wheel. She resumed driving, a grimace on her face.

"Those tentacles really are disgusting," he said, trying to ease the tension.

"Harold is disgusting," said Lana with venom.

"How'd you get stuck with him?" asked Darius.

"Let's just focus on the task at hand, okay?" said Lana. "Can we do that?"

"Okay," said Darius as he turned his eyes to the road.

Several blocks passed by in awkward silence before Lana once again pulled the car to the curb. She pointed across the street to a bar called "The Civil Disagreement". The sign for the bar flashed neon, and showed a muscular man with a frown shaking his head. The sign looked more expensive then the building itself, as its graffiti covered walls were spotted with large cracks and dings. The name struck Darius as a little too clever for Cassius's tastes. Perhaps he hadn't given the bastard enough credit in the intellect department… or maybe the man just liked the shiny lights and dingy atmosphere. Either way, according to Harold, this was "Jamal's" favorite haunt. They would find him here.

"You go first. Find a spot at the bar. Order a drink," said Lana. "Then I'll sit at the bar. You ask if you can buy me a drink. We'll let him come to us."

"Got it," said Darius, opening his car door.

"And Darius," said Lana.

"Yeah?" he said.

"Do *not* speak to him until I get there. You follow my lead," said Lana, forcefully.

Darius grunted, then nodded. He stepped out of the car, and shut the door behind himself. He stood on the sidewalk as the car pulled away. His pulse quickened and he clenched his fists. Confession or not, Lana was planning on making the arrest tonight. An arrest would put Cassius just out of reach for much longer than Darius was willing to wait. He had to make his move.

He took a deep breath in, then moved across the street. He reached the door and pulled it open. Lynyrd Skynyrd faintly played on ancient speakers. Cigarette smoke flowed into his nose as he stepped further in. He peered through the haze to see rows of vacant, splintering wooden tables. A few tired old men sat in various corners, drinking to their sorrows, but the only man who caught Darius's eye sat hunched at the end of the long bar, halfway through a Jack & Coke. Cassius did not look up as Darius climbed onto a stool six seats away.

His hand started to quiver with anxiety. This could be his last chance, had his backup arrived? Darius switched to infrared, and glanced about the bar again. Not a tentacle could be seen. *Shit.*

"What are you having?"

Darius jumped a bit and turned to the bar. A large, gruff, bearded man was tending it. "I'll have a…" said Darius, desperately trying to think of a drink, "Get me a Shirley Temple."

The bartender guffawed. "Shirley Temple? Hey Jamal,

get a load of this kid."

Shit, thought Darius. *I thought that was a real drink. Should have stuck with club soda.*

Cassius looked up from his Jack & Coke, his eyes slightly swimming. "What'd you say Wilson?"

"This kid just ordered a fucking Shirley Temple," shouted Wilson, still chortling.

Cassius raised an eyebrow at Darius, before saying, "A Shirley Temple? You a nancy boy or something?"

Cassius's juvenile jibe sounded another round of laughs from Wilson. Darius steeled his jaw and clenched his fist on the bar. *Better not back down.*

"I ordered my drink," said Darius. "Are you going to make it or not?"

Wilson laughed again, "Well I'm sorry, *honey*, the Civil Disagreement doesn't carry grenadine."

Cassius chimed in, "There's a gay bar down the street, if you're looking for fruit."

Wilson's chuckling doubled again. Darius's blood began to boil. He glanced around the bar. Most of the men were keeping to themselves, but none of those men were the Cuttlefish. *Where the fuck is he...*

"Just get me a beer then," grumbled Darius. "Whatever you've got on tap."

"A beer huh?" said Wilson, smile on his face. "I can do that, but just to be clear, our beer contains alcohol."

"If you're looking for root beer, try Toys R Us," Cassius chimed in.

Wilson doubled over in laughter. *That dumbass joke doesn't even make sense*, thought Darius.

A creak sounded through the bar as the front door opened. Darius turned to see Lana enter the building. *Damn it*, he thought. He then noticed she was wearing more revealing clothing than she was in the car… and more leather. *Damn.*

All eyes turned to Lana as she calmly strutted to the bar. Darius saw her shoot him a glare when she noticed the laughing men, but she quickly returned to character, and sat down between him and Cassius. Neither of the men could take their eyes off her.

Wilson perked up at the sight of Lana, and caught his breath before saying, "Well hello darling. What are you having tonight?"

Lana crossed her legs and leaned forward on the bar. "I'm not sure yet. I suppose I'll drink whatever's paid for." She then slyly looked left and right.

She's good at this, thought Darius. He might have spoken up, even if it hadn't been his line. "I could buy a drink, in exchange for conversation."

Wilson started to giggle, but Cassius was the first to speak. "You don't want what he's buying miss. He just wants you to lick his pussy."

Wilson shook with laughter, and Cassius grinned smugly. Lana raised an eyebrow at Darius as he glared at the bastard. She then turned to Cassius, "Does that mean you'll buy me something better?"

"Wilson, get her an Old Fashioned," Cassius stood up and sauntered over next to Lana, "because I'm an Old Fashioned kind of guy."

"What if I'm looking for something a little more modern?" asked Lana, glancing towards Darius.

He stood up to move closer and started to speak, "I can…"

"I'm not sure Shirley Temple qualifies as modern," interrupted Cassius.

Wilson chortled, and Darius stopped in his tracks.

"Shirley Temple?" asked Lana, looking at Darius with genuine surprise.

"Yes ma'am," said Cassius. "That's his... sorry, her drink of choice."

Wilson cracked up. Darius tensed his fist. Lana started to smile herself. She said, "A Shirley Temple, huh?"

Frown on his face, Darius stated firmly, "A real man drinks what he likes."

Cassius responded, "A real man likes women."

Even Lana started to giggle at that crack. Darius's anger was building to a dangerous level. "Do you know what I do for a living?" he asked.

"Suck dick?" responded Cassius, laughter ensuing.

"I weld," said Darius. "I bend and shape massive chunks of metal to my will with the scorching heat of a flame that only I control. What the fuck do you do, huh? Sit on your ass making dumbass jokes? Which of us is more of a man?"

In their giddy haze, Cassius and Wilson failed to notice Darius's genuine fury. Only Lana, knowing Darius's relation with Cassius, noticed the emotional weight behind his tantrum. She attempted to defuse the situation.

"You're a welder?" she asked. "I hear welders make a lot of money. Money pays for drinks, like... whiskey?"

Lana's interjection pulled Darius back into the situation. His anger had almost gotten the better of him. He turned to Wilson and said, "A whiskey for the lady."

Cassius frowned at Lana's persistence towards the younger man, but it was Wilson who spoke first. "Alright son," said Wilson. "I'll need to see your ID."

Darius reached for his pocket before he heard Cassius chuckle. This made Darius indignant. "Seriously? You're going to card me in a shit-hole like this?"

"The law's the law," said Wilson.

Fuming, Darius reached for his pocket again. His pocket was empty. He patted his sides, looking for his wallet. It was nowhere to be found. He looked at Wilson who was clearly stifling a grin.

"I'm afraid my ID has gone missing," said Darius, suspicious.

Wilson responded, holding back a chuckle, "I guess you'll just have to leave."

Darius stared at Wilson. He glanced at Lana, who shrugged, then looked at Cassius, a smug grin on his face.

Darius could feel his fists heating up.

"You want to know what I do for a living, kid?" asked Cassius. "Whatever I damn well please."

Lana perked up. Darius ground his teeth.

"If I want to sleep, I sleep. If I want to drink, I drink," continued Cassius. "If I want to buy a pretty lady a drink, I buy her a drink. I don't even have to use my own money…" Cassius pulled Darius's wallet out from his own pocket and placed it on the bar. "If I don't want to."

Darius clenched his fists and edged closer to Cassius. Lana didn't notice, as she focused on getting what she came for.

"Wow," said Lana, eyes going wide, "how'd you do that? Are you a street magician or something?"

"I'm no magician," said Cassius, leaning in towards Lana, "but I can do magical things."

"If you want to?" asked Lana, licking her lips.

"If I want to," said Cassius.

Darius tapped Cassius on the shoulder, his finger emitting an intense heat. The bastard's eyes narrowed as he turned to look at Darius standing over him.

"I think I know something Wilson wants to do," said

Darius, pointing at Wilson. "Check my ID."

Wilson reached for the wallet, but Cassius quickly held up his hand to stop him. Cassius slowly turned, picked up the wallet, and pulled out the ID.

Lana's eyes went wide and stammered a quick attempt to stall the situation, "Now come on guys, is this really necessary?"

"Quiet woman," snapped Cassius. He lifted the ID into his vision, his frown deepening. He glanced at Darius, glanced at the ID, and froze. His breath staggered, fear overcoming him.

Darius smiled and leaned in close, bearing over him. He said with a low and grumbling voice, "Hello, Cassius."

Cassius's head shook back and forth, overwhelmed with panic. "No," he said. "No you can't... there's no way... you couldn't find me..."

"Sure about that?" asked Darius. Feeling the power of the moment, he channeled his fury into his eyes, igniting them into bright and terrifying flames.

"No!" shouted Cassius, his body moving too fast to see.

FWOOOMP!

Darius flew across the room, crashing against the back wall. The impact stunned him, and his chest throbbed with the pain of a foot crashing into it.

Cassius leapt to his feet and screamed, "Fuck! Off!"

Before Lana could lift her hand, the front door had blasted open with a deafening crash, and Cassius was gone.

Chapter 5
THE PENULTIMATE PUNCH

Darius struggled to his feet, the fire in his eyes put out by the pain of the impact. He looked up to see a bar nearly abandoned. Lana was the only person in view, and she made quite the sight.

Lana's hands glowed a deep blue, brandished towards Darius. Her eyes were filled with determination and betrayal, and they held fierce with his. Even her hair, flowing down her shoulders in sheen waves, seemed set on keeping him down.

"You called him Cassius," said Lana.

Darius coughed. "That's his name."

"Who is he?" asked Lana.

"A dead man," said Darius. He coughed again, then spat some blood on the ground. He wiped his mouth with his arm.

"He's just a thief," said Lana. "What did he take from you that could be so important?"

"My mother," said Darius.

Lana's blue glow faded as she took a deep breath in and let a deep breath out. "Have you heard of forgiveness?" she asked.

"I've heard of it," said Darius. "Don't really see the point."

"It's great," said Lana. "It helps you move past things like that."

"Forgive *me* if I don't give a shit."

Lana sighed. "I don't think you have a choice. I can't

just let you kill him, and I can't just let you walk away."

"Uh-huh," said Darius, his hands igniting into flame.

Lana's eyes flashed, and she snapped her hands together, glowing blue with an intense brilliance. Massive hands made of an immaterial blue light appeared in the air, wrapping Darius in a psychic force-field, pinning his arms against his body.

Darius wriggled in place, struggling to catch his breath against the crushing weight of Lana's grip. In desperation, he called his anger forward and felt it building in the pit of his stomach. He shouted to the world, "I always have a choice!"

KABOOOOOOOOM.

The bar trembled beneath the awesome power of Darius's eruption. Lana's massive hands contained most of the fiery blast, but the shockwave from the explosion battered the walls of the building, and knocked Lana to the ground. Her concentration faltered and her hands vanished, allowing Darius to collapse to his knees.

Breathing heavily, he slowly got to his feet. Lana rolled on the floor, hands on her forehead, blood dripping from her nose.

Looking at her pain, Darius felt a tinge of regret. He had never wanted to hurt a woman. Part of him wanted to stop. To comfort her. To apologize. But Cassius was getting away.

He got to his feet and slogged to the doorway, each step laborious. The open frame and shattered wood looked strikingly similar to the liquor store two days earlier. He determined to follow this path wherever it led.

Just as he started to step through the door, a weak and flickering wall of blue light appeared in his way. He turned around to see Lana crouched on one knee, struggling to hold up her hand.

"I can't... I can't just let you leave..." she stammered.

Darius frowned. "You don't have a choice."

He held up his hand and spewed a vicious stream of flame directly towards Lana. Her eyes went wide in fright, and the wall vanished from the doorway before reappearing between Lana and the flames.

"AAAAAGGGGHHHHHH," screamed Lana, as she used all the energy she had to shield herself from the raging fire. Darius did not relent.

Her screams started to fade and the wall began to flicker. Tears streamed down her face, and her screams soon turned to sobs. Her wall faded away, and Lana collapsed to the ground with a nearly silent, "no...".

Darius cut the flames. She could not stop him now. With one last look at her face, newly red with singed off eyebrows, he stepped through the broken door and into the night street.

His ears were greeted by shrill sirens, blaring throughout the streets. Instead of the "Wees" and "Woos" of police, these sirens wailed with the sound of impending disaster, accompanied by a monotonous computerized warning, "Supers in combat. Put on your helmets." The Coalition's warning signaled eventual reinforcements. Darius was running out of time.

He switched his eyes to infrared and glanced at the ground. Iridescent footprints led down the street, back in the direction of Cassius's home. If Darius was lucky, the bastard would still be there packing his things. Glass bottles can only be loaded so quickly.

Darius took off, sprinting down the street. His feet lined up with the prints in the road, legs bounding with unearthly force and determination. Still, the footprints started to fade, and his lungs began to fail. He would again need a car.

Looking back and forth, he saw only barren streets. Not a single headlight accompanied the streetlights, and not a single horn could be heard among the sirens. Darius knew that in the city proper, even Supers could not stop traffic, but here in Old Town people took the sirens seriously. If he cared about politics, he would have known of the controversy surrounding the Coalition's treatment of impoverished communities. In the city, the Coalition did their best to keep fights contained, but in Old Town, Supers could go buck-wild with rampant destruction. Nobody would force them to pay for the damages. These policies held many implications for Darius's situation, but in the moment, it only struck him as a nuisance. It wasn't for another two blocks before a car approached him on the road.

Darius spotted the headlights, put himself in their path, and placed his feet firmly on the ground. The car barreled down the road with its own sense of energy, showing no sign of slowing. He let his hands ignite. When the flames appeared, the car's brakes screeched, bringing the vehicle to a grinding halt just in front of him. He marched toward the driver's door prepared to tear the driver from the car, but the driver stuck his head out the window and shouted, "Get in the car!"

Stunned, Darius let his flames go out. He looked at the driver with confusion. An angry, chubby, and pale face looked back at him. It took a second for him to recognize the tentacle-less Cuttlefish shouting at him.

"Get in here!" yelled the Cuttlefish.

"Where the fuck were you?" Darius screamed back, climbing into the backseat.

"I was there," said the Cuttlefish, foot returning to the gas pedal, "And I saw everything."

"No, Harold," said Darius, "You weren't there when I fucking needed you. You fucked up, and now he's getting away."

"You never should have given him your ID," said the Cuttlefish.

"I didn't give it to him, he took it," replied Darius.

"And you pushed him to read it," said the Cuttlefish. "I could have stung him easy if you hadn't pressed him."

"You should have stung him before he even knew I was there," said Darius.

"I've got my own things going on, alright? I thought I'd have more time," said the Cuttlefish.

"Bullshit," said Darius. "You were probably just watching Lana change."

The Cuttlefish blushed beet red. He mumbled, "I was seeing where she parked the car."

For the first time, Darius noticed the interior of the car was familiar to him. They were driving Lana's car, and the keys were in the ignition. *He must have grabbed the keys off her when I ran out the door,* thought Darius.

"Whatever you say, Harold," he said, "Just get me to his house."

The Cuttlefish cleared his throat, "Burn my chip, and I'll take you."

"That wasn't the deal," said Darius. "You were supposed to knock him out. You didn't. The chip stays in, and you're taking me to him."

"Only if you burn my chip," said the Cuttlefish.

Darius leaned forward behind the Cuttlefish's ear. "Don't fuck with me, Harold. I'm going after him. If you stand in my way, I won't hesitate to put you down."

Just then, Darius felt a sharp pain in his neck. His eyes tracked downwards to see an invisible stinger wax into view. The appendage looked even more disgusting than usual, snaked around the side of the Cuttlefish's face and stabbed into Darius's neck.

The Cuttlefish managed to speak with a slight muddling, "I won't hesitate either. Burn the chip, and I'll take you to him."

Darius's fury was filling to the brim. He wanted nothing more than to engulf the car in flames, incinerating the Cuttlefish along with his stinger, but the squid-boy wasn't his real target. The fucker had fucked him over, and was going to get away with it.

"Fuck!" shouted Darius. He slowly leaned back, and removed the headrest from the seat in front of him, revealing the back of the Cuttlefish's neck. "Hold still, asshole. This is going to hurt."

Darius switched his vision to infrared. The chip maintained the same temperature as the Cuttlefish's body, but the signal it broadcast added a slight, almost imperceptible motion to the heat waves coming from the chip. He could tell approximately how deep it was, and how hot he had to burn to get it. At least the Cuttlefish had to suffer with him.

Darius lifted his index finger up to the bump in the Cuttlefish's neck, holding it slightly off of the skin. He focused his ire into the point of his finger with the technique and precision he'd mastered through years of welding, and released a concentrated flame directly into the squid-boy's neck.

The Cuttlefish shrieked, his neck and the car swerving. Darius moved his finger with the chip, relishing the pain he inflicted and ignoring the sharp pain of the stinger wriggling in his own neck.

"Are you done?" The Cuttlefish cried. Darius knew the chip had melted almost immediately after he started the flame, but the sight of the squid-boy's crackling flesh had kept the flame on his finger.

"Almost!" shouted Darius a grin growing on his face.

CRASH.

The window next to Darius shattered, cascading into the vehicle. Instinctively, he turned the flame on his finger towards the open window and let the focused jet spread into a wide stream of fire. A flash of movement to his left caught his eye. He looked through the rearview window to see Cassius holding a metal bat, keeping pace with the car.

"He's here!" shouted Darius.

Tears streaming down his face, Harold retracted the stinger from Darius's neck back into his mouth. He muttered something unintelligible then wiped some tears from his face. He started to speed the car up, so Darius took that as a good sign that he was listening.

Darius shouted out the window at the top of his lungs, "You finally stop running, you old fucker?"

With two quick steps, Cassius vanished and the frame of the car door bent inward with a hard metallic CLANG. Cassius reappeared trailing behind the vehicle, a new ding in his bat. It was his turn to show off.

Darius nodded. This was it. The showdown he had always dreamed of.

"Roll down the windows and step on the gas," he instructed the still bawling Harold. As the yet unbroken windows started to lower, Darius moved himself to the center of the backseat, legs curled up in front of him, facing Cassius. He raised his hands into full view of the rear window, lifted his middle fingers, and let them ignite in flame. He called it "The Double Phoenix", and it had never felt so gratifying.

Cassius held the bat to the ground, sparks flying into the air.

Go time.

Cassius flashed out of sight. Darius whipped his flaming fingers to the sides. A CLANG and a cave-in on the right rear car door were met with jets of flame pouring out the backseat windows.

Coughs sounded in the air, and Darius saw Cassius reappear, losing ground to the car, coughing into his arm. Darius cut his flames.

"The next time you hear a clang, ram him," Darius told Harold.

"Just... swerve?" asked Harold, through his tears.

"Ram him, swerve at him, whatever!" shouted Darius. "Just hit him with the fucking car!"

"How will I know he's coming?" asked Harold, taking a sharp right turn. The chase had brought them further into the area of Old Town filled with defunct factories. The Super sirens wailed softer here, but the roads were just as clear.

"I'll fucking tell you!" shouted Darius as he watched Cassius slowly regain his composure, still on their tail. The bastard coughed once more, then stood up straight. Darius watched him lift his bat, and tighten his grip.

"He's coming!" shouted Darius, shortly preceding another CLANG which saw the back right door torn off its hinges.

Harold jerked the steering wheel hard to the right. A wail sounded from the road, and Cassius's blurred figure reappeared as he stumbled at the side of the road, somersaulting on the ground.

"Don't stop driving," shouted Darius as he climbed to the now open doorway. He formed a ball of fire in his hand and flung it at the rolling Cassius.

Darius thought he saw Cassius's eyes go wide as he leapt to avoid the ball of flame. The bastard cleared the blast, but struggled to regain his footing, tripping across the concrete. Darius flung another ball, and then another, Cassius leaping over both, slowly regaining control step by step.

Darius knew he probably wouldn't be able to hit him, but seeing the bastard's persistence in avoiding the fire gave him inspiration. *If I can't hit him, maybe I can...*

Darius stuck both his hands out of the open doorway, and let loose a plume of fire from each. He aimed one plume toward the ground at Cassius's feet, and kept the other aimed at the ground directly to the side of the car. As the bastard worked to avoid the fire pointed at him, a wake of flames formed beneath the speeding vehicle. The leaping and stumbling Cassius didn't notice as he was led by the fire to follow directly behind the car.

Darius began crossing the pillars of flame, forcing the bastard to jump over the plumes to avoid incineration. Darius shouted up to Harold, "When I shout 'now', slam on the brakes!"

"I don't... I don't know if that's such a good idea..." said Harold.

"Do it or die, you piece of shit!" shouted Darius.

"Okay..." mumbled Harold.

Darius slowly brought his hands together. The fire pillars started to spin and fuse together, forming a tunnel of flames surrounding Cassius, fusing shut behind him. Inch by inch, the fire crept closer to the bastard, and the only way out was forward.

Darius watched as a drenched-in-sweat Cassius leaned forward and took a deep breath in. Darius smiled and shouted, "Now!"

As Harold's foot slammed on the brakes, the car began screeching to a grinding halt. The rear window shattered and the trunk flew open as Cassius collided with the back of the car. His body spilled across the vehicle and tumbled across the pavement, eventually rolling to a stop 100 feet ahead of the vehicle.

Darius's torso crashed against the jagged edge of a torn door hinge, and his head slammed against the ground, grinding on the pavement, tearing apart his scalp. The impact would have killed a normal human.

Instead, the blinding pain pulled from Darius a level of power he had not seen since his powers first awakened. Consumed by agony, his body erupted into flames. For a quick shimmer of time his corporeal form was subsumed by ethereal fire, emitting a hellish shriek that echoed across the deserted roads.

Harold watched in horror as Darius's awesome power faded as quickly as it had erupted, and a naked and mended Darius climbed to his feet and crawled into the back seat of the car.

"Drive me to him," said Darius.

Speechless, Harold pulled the car towards a battered Cassius who was struggling to stand.

"Line him up with the back door," said Darius.

Wordlessly, Harold obeyed. Just as Cassius got to his feet, the car pulled up beside him, and Darius placed his own feet against the inside of the door. With a push and a blast, he blew it off its hinges and into the bastard, flinging him through the air and crashing him into the wall of a factory across the street.

The car door fell to the ground, and Cassius fell on top of it. Darius climbed out of the car and made his way to him.

Darius popped his knuckles as he approached the bastard who was bruised and bloodied on the ground. Cassius's eyes looked up in panic and terror as Darius leaned over him.

"I'm not done with you yet," said Darius, reaching down and grabbing Cassius by the nape of his neck. Tears started to fall from his eyes as Darius dragged him back to the car.

Harold was standing behind the car staring into the trunk with a worried look. When Darius reached Harold, he said, "Sting him, quick."

Harold glanced at Cassius, then glanced back in the trunk. He opened his mouth and the stinger slithered out, wriggling with a sickening motion. As the stinger found a spot in Cassius's neck, the bastard vomited across the ground, blood mixing with bile.

Darius didn't notice Cassius fall unconscious in his hand. His eyes were now locked on the trunk of the car, where his gaze had just found Lana lying unconscious with breasts stripped bare. He now knew what the Cuttlefish was, and he was surprised with how disgusted he could be with a man who had not been his step-father.

"Do you want me to drive you somewhere?" asked the Cuttlefish, terrified by the power before him.

Darius's heart shook with guilt as he stared at Lana's broken form. He would never be able to make this right again.

He looked at the Cuttlefish with a gaze that could kill from fear alone. As the Cuttlefish withered beneath his stare, Darius said, "I want you dead. But right now, I've got bigger fish to fry."

Darius picked up Cassius's limp body and put him across his shoulder. As he walked towards the nearest factory, decrepit and crumbling in the dark of the night, a tear escaped Darius's eye.

Forgive me.

Chapter 6
THE
BALEFUL
BLAZE

Cassius woke up screaming. He was in pain.

For the first time in years, Cassius felt pain. Real, physical, pain.

He reached for a drink. Instead of the bottle he kept on his bedside table, his hand found only air above a concrete floor.

He slammed his fist against the ground. The rough concrete scraped his skin, but that pain paled in comparison to the pounding in his head, the bruised soreness of his torso, the almost overwhelming burning in his right ankle, and most of all, the petulant thirst for the only thing that made his life bearable.

Cassius strained to open his eyes, only to realize that his eyes were already open. He was surrounded by darkness and had woken up on a concrete bed at the bottom of an abyss. It may as well have been The Abyss, for he began to fear that he would never see the light of day again.

As shitty as his life had been, Cassius was sure that whatever came next could only get worse. He decided to rise to his feet.

Fighting through the aches and soreness, Cassius rolled over and pulled his knees beneath him. He planted his left foot squarely on the ground and tried to stand. As he placed weight on his right leg, his ankle was shot with a stabbing and burning pain unlike anything he had ever felt before.

Screams renewed, and he collapsed to the floor, tears streaming down his face. In the darkness he reached for his foo-… he reached for his f-… his foot was no longer there. Instead, his hands found a cauterized stump of flesh where his ankle should have been, grimy flesh and oozy pus rubbed onto his palms.

"Looking for this?" rumbled a voice in the darkness.

Cassius heard something fly through the air before it thudded against his chest, and landed in his lap. He picked up the object. The cold of its skin shocked him more than its broken toes and charred top. He held his severed foot. He sobbed.

"If I had more time, I would have made you eat it," said the voice.

"That's sick!" blurted Cassius as he cradled his foot in his arms. "You're sick!"

Chuckles emanated from the darkness. Darius replied, "You're one to talk."

"You don't know me…" muttered Cassius.

"On the contrary," said Darius, "I think I'm the only person alive who knows you."

"Bullshit!" shouted Cassius. "You have no clue the stuff I've been through, no fucking clue! You don't know my life, and you don't know me! Don't try coming in here and telling me *my* story."

"I don't need to know your story to tell you how it ends," said Darius. Two small flames the size of eyeballs appeared in the air, twenty feet away.

"Fuck you!" shouted Cassius, hurling his severed foot towards the flames.

The sound of flesh hitting flesh echoed through the room. The acrid smell of burning meat soon followed as Cassius's foot combusted, lighting the room in an eerie glow. Skin and muscle sloughed off the foot in Darius's fiery palm, disintegrating into ash. Darius's twisted smile and persistent gaze made Cassius sweat more than the intense heat that filled the room. Cassius could see no mercy in the flames.

In the muted and terrifying light, the cold concrete walls felt even more imposing than the pure darkness that came before. However, unlike the darkness, the walls had gaps. The walls had an escape.

Calling on his power, Cassius twisted to his knees and crawled at an inhuman speed, bursting towards the nearest doorway. The new room was hardly lit through the doorway behind Cassius, but he could just barely make out the silhouette of a tiered, square staircase climbing upwards. Cassius labored up the first flight only to collapse on the landing as his lungs gasped for air.

Cassius strained to catch his breath as the room slowly grew brighter and brighter, a low chuckle resonating through the air. Cassius glanced back to the door to see Darius saunter into the frame, both hands ablaze.

"You'll need to move a hell of a lot faster than that," said Darius, "if you want to live."

Cassius took a deep breath in, then burst away, crawling up two more flights of stairs before collapsing again. Even if his chest hadn't ached from rampant bruising, the heat in the air made it almost unbearably stifling to breathe. The concrete walls not only acted as a prison; they formed an oven.

A ball of fire flew above Cassius's head and burst against the wall. Darius's voice echoed from below, "Faster!"

Cassius needed to get out. He looked up to see the staircase extending at least ten stories further. If he could make it to the roof he could escape the heat, but at this rate, he would never reach it. He had to find another way.

He burst up another flight of stairs and through a doorway onto the second floor. He slammed the door behind him and leaned against it, trying to catch his breath. A hallway stretched before him, and doors to various rooms lined the walls on either side. At the end of the hallway, dim fluorescent light leaked in. The sickly yellow of streetlights had never looked so inviting to Cassius. He took another deep breath in before crawling towards the light.

As he sped to the end of the hallway, he glanced at the doors at his sides. Their bulky metal frames were rough and strangely shaped, and as he approached the light he could better see them. Each door had been welded shut.

Cassius crawled headlong into the room at the end of the hall before he realized the implications of a forced pathway. The door slammed shut behind him, trapping Cassius in a small room with several streams of outside light leaking in. The windows that lined the wall, had been closed off with makeshift bars welded from machine parts which had been abandoned in the factory. Some of the light that leaked into the room was being directed with molded metal into a single word which stretched across the floor: BLEED.

Tears mixed with the sweat that dripped into Cassius's eyes. *I've got to get away...*

Light started to build in the room. Cassius looked up to see a portion of the ceiling glowing a hot white. The concrete above him started to crumble and disintegrate. A hole formed, and an unbearably intense heat filled the room.

Cassius pushed himself against the wall, panting while

he watched as a flame-swathed Darius dropped to the floor before him. Through the fire, Cassius could see a wide and horrifying smile spread across Darius's face.

Darius inched towards Cassius, an axe made from concentrated heat and flame forming in his hands. Cassius's eyes darted across the room. The only way out was up.

Darius raised his axe to swing, and Cassius bolted out behind him, forcing himself to move through the explosive pain of weight placed on his amputated foot. He leapt with supernatural speed up through the hole. His chest cleared the floor, and in the split second before his body began to fall, Cassius saw stenciled light cast across this floor as well; "BLEED".

He's got the whole building locked down... thought Cassius. He raised his hands to grab the concrete ledge in order to stop his fall.

His palms connected. He screeched.

Reflexively, he let go of the ledge, his hands singed and puffy after only a millisecond of contact. He fell to the ground, cradling his hands against his chest, blood seeping from the wound on his ankle.

Darius turned around and stood over Cassius with the flaming axe raised above his head. He said, "Which one next?"

In fear, Cassius kicked at Darius. Even flying at mach speed, his foot could not outpace the flames surrounding his captor. Darius stood unfazed, and Cassius's foot returned to the ground with brand new blisters boiling upon his skin.

Tears streamed out of Cassius's eyes and evaporated before crossing his cheeks. "Isn't this enough?" He screamed holding up his stump. "Haven't you done enough?"

"Let's find out," said Darius.

Darius swung the axe downwards. Instinctively, Cassius raised his hands in defense. Unfortunately, hands cannot properly defend against an axe made of fire.

The axe seared its way through Cassius's left wrist, lopping off his hand and half of his forearm. Cassius's brain erupted with neurons firing off in chemical distress. He screamed.

Darius lowered his axe and waited for Cassius's shrieks to subside. "Hmm," he said, "not enough. It's just not enough."

"Fuck you!" shouted Cassius, roiling from the pain. "Why... why couldn't you just let me be? Why couldn't you just leave me alone? After all these years... all these goddamn years..."

Darius turned away from Cassius and moved to the door. He lifted his open hand and blasted the door off its hinges. He stepped to the side of the door and motioned his hand towards the open doorway. "Maybe you can earn a few more years."

"Fuck. You!" shouted Cassius.

"Okay," said Darius raising his axe above his head and moving back towards Cassius.

"No!" shouted Cassius. He pushed himself away from Darius with his "good" foot, wailing and writhing on the ground. "No, no, no, no, no!"

Cassius's back bumped up against the wall, and Darius brought the axe cutting down a second time.

Cassius's right arm plopped onto the floor, severed just below his shoulder.

The burst of pain overwhelmed Cassius's consciousness. He could think only of the searing pain that consumed him and the act that had brought this fury down upon him. When Darius raised his axe a third time, a flash of adrenaline and instinct brought Cassius halfway through the hallway. Another flash brought him back to the stairwell, leaning on the stump of his ankle, blood oozing from the wound.

Cassius's heart ached. Everything he thought he had left behind, everything he had drowned out, everything he had tried to drink away… everything was coming back. His past was catching up with him. But… he could run a little further.

In a blur of time and flesh, Cassius made his way up eight stories worth of stairs. He leaned against the railing looking up towards the exit. It was so close, but his body was nearing its quitting point. The blood-loss was starting to take its toll. He didn't think he could make it.

A low rumble sounded from below Cassius in the stairway. He looked down to see Darius's grinning face slowly ascending towards him on a pillar of flame.

He didn't think he could make it… but he had to try.

Tearing through the pain that tore through him, Cassius fought his way up the last two stories step-by-step. Each high-velocity step pounded his burned foot or his bloody stump against the ground, exposed bone now grinding against the concrete. He reached the door labeled "roof access" and pushed it open. A cool breeze brushed against his face as he stumbled into the night sky. It was the greatest feeling he had ever felt, but it wasn't enough to keep him on his feet.

Cassius collapsed face down on the ground, blood seeping from his missing limbs. He looked at the sky. The faint glow of dawn greeted his eyes. *Almost… there…*

Cassius took a deep breath in before wriggling his

broken body, moving millimeters at a time across the ground. He glanced towards the sky again.

The glow seemed off. It wasn't coming from the sky.

With great effort, Cassius lifted his head to look towards the center of the roof. The concrete emanated a bright white heat.

I'm... fucked.

In a glorious blast of heat and light, the concrete of the roof disintegrated into nothingness, and a massive pillar of flame stretched high into the sky, consuming the factory.

The building began to shake, and walls and floors started to collapse, falling to the center of the great mass of flame. Cassius watched helplessly as a snakelike swathe of glowing fury cut through the mass of concrete he lay upon and carried it to the center of the conflagration.

The fire raged around him in seeming chaos, but none touched him directly, parting before him so he could reach the source. Reach his "son".

Darius stood at the base of the building, lava flowing beneath his feet. His body was composed of an ethereal glow; only his face remained vaguely human.

Cassius watched as Darius lifted his fiery arms and his flaming hand seethed through the air. The hand clasped around Cassius good leg, burning it out of existence. Cassius would have screamed, but he simply didn't have the energy.

Darius moved forward and leaned down to Cassius's face to look him directly in the eyes.

A croaking and crackling voice emanated from Darius's maw, "It's still not enough."

One last tear fell from Cassius's eye and he shook with sobs. "You know I... I never..." stammered a breathless Cassius, "I never meant to kill her..."

Darius's fiery gaze was uncompromising. The demonic voice echoed out, "I know."

Darius's human visage melted away, overtaken by a terrible and burning face of fire. He opened his mouth wide.

Cassius, limbless and lying in an evaporated pool of his own blood, closed his eyes and let out one last sob as his body, his essence, his being, was swallowed by the flames.

THE
SMOLDERING
RUINS

Darius stood naked in the center of a crater. The shrieks and cries of the area's populace were overpowered by the wail of fire truck sirens sounding in the distance, coming to fight the fire that had spread to the surrounding factories. The blaze that roared around him was wild and unkempt, but the lava beneath his feet had finally hardened. Water and sewer mains destroyed in the blaze had started to flood the area with runoff and sludge, dampening the heat that clung to the air.

Darius closed his eyes and clenched his fists. He won. Over a decade of hunting and he had finally caught his quarry. He imagined the pride Kiyana must feel, smiling down at her son. It was over.

It was over…

A booming voice echoed through the crater, "Darius Snipes."

Darius opened his eyes. A muscular man in pearly white combat armor hovered ten feet off the ground above the edge of the crater. A deep blue "W" stretched across his chest.

Darius smirked. The indomitable man, "Mr. Invincible", Worldpower, himself, had come to stop him, and he was too late.

"By the authority of the Carthage Coalition of Superhumans, I am placing you under arrest," said Worldpower. "You have the right to remain silent…"

Darius had never given much thought to what came after the hunt. Prison had always seemed likely. Now it seemed more likely than ever. However, if the Coalition used a shit-bag like the Cuttlefish...

Maybe, thought Darius, *maybe they'll let me fight. I'll have to come up with a name.*

He glanced at the hardened lava cooling beneath his feet. *The Molten Man? No, too long and too... comic-booky.*

His eyes noticed the ash floating about in the air around him. *Cinder? That sounds kind of cool, but cinders are the left-overs. They're out. They're weak.*

He moved to look at the blaze subsuming the surrounding neighborhoods, but something closer by caught his attention. At the edge of the crater, smoke and a hot orange glow radiated from a charred and ashen telephone pole, burning without flames.

Smolder? Nah... well... Smolder. Huh.

Darius smiled.

Smolder.

COMING SOON...

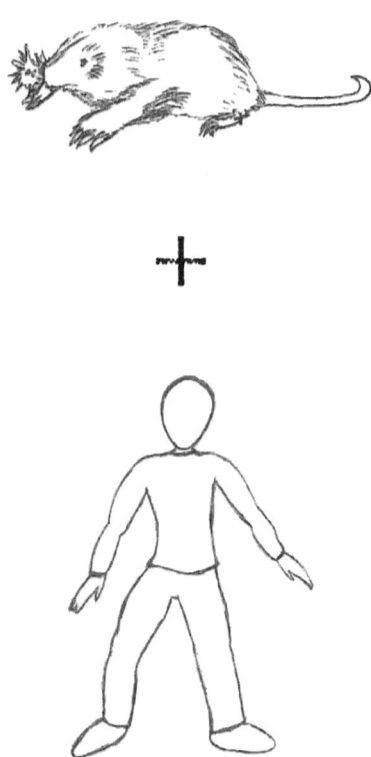